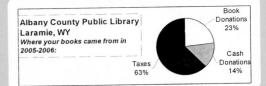

A STORY

with Pictures

STORY BY: BARBARA KANNINEN

PICTURES BY: LYNN ROWE REED

Story with Pictures
by Barbara Kanninen
Illustrated by Lynn Rowe Reed
Holiday House/New York

dedications to come

text copyright © 2007 by Barbara Kanninen
illustrations copyright © 2007 by Lynn Rowe Reed
All Rights Reserved
The text face is
The illustrations were done in
Printed in the United States of America / Manufactured in China
www.holidayhouse.com
1 3 5 7 9 10 8 6 4 2
Library of Congress Cataloging in publication data to come
First Edition

Page 3
Hi there. I am the author of A STORY WITH PICTURES.
I hope you like this book!

Page 4
Ack! Where are the pictures? This is supposed to be A STORY WITH
PICTURES, not a story WITHOUT pictures. It says so right here in my
manuscript.

the illustrator. How will she know what to put in

Page 1 of 5

Holiday House / New York

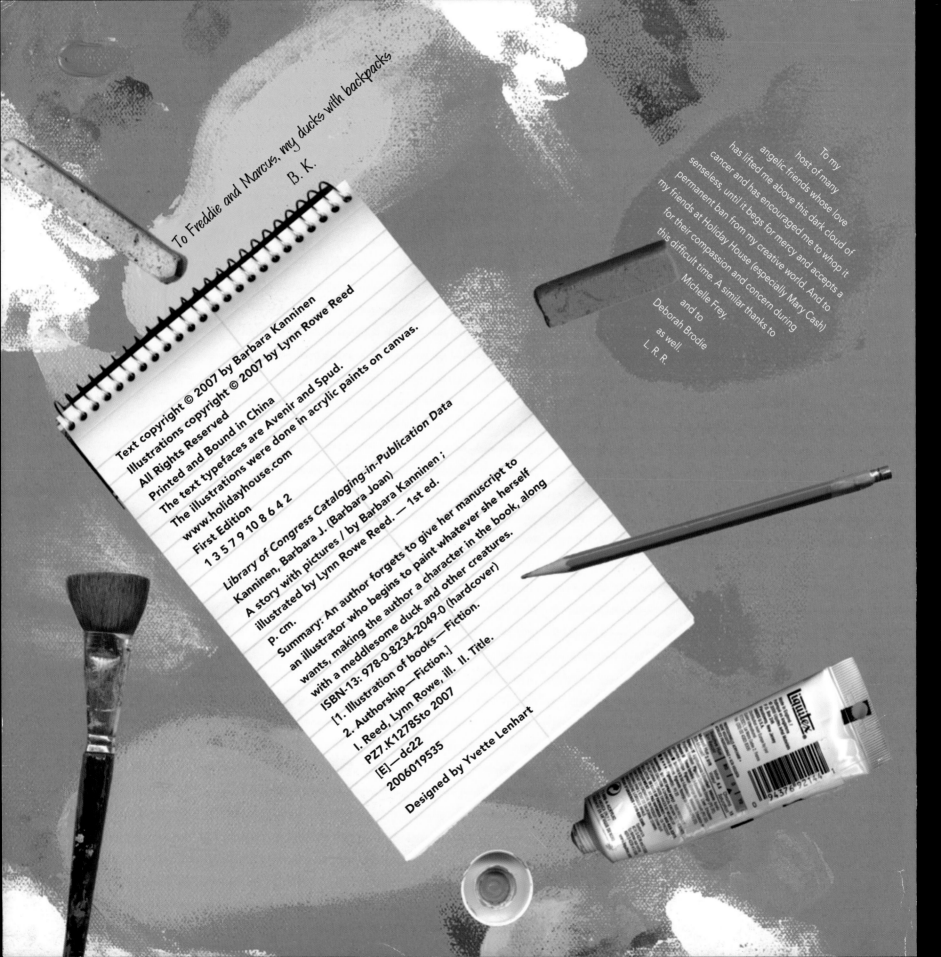

To Freddie and Marcus, my ducks with backpacks.
B. K.

To my
host of many
angelic friends whose love
has lifted me above this dark cloud of
cancer and has encouraged me to whop it
senseless, until it begs for mercy and accepts a
permanent ban from my creative world. And to
my friends at Holiday House (especially Mary Cash)
for their compassion and concern during
this difficult time. A similar thanks to
Michelle Frey,
and to
Deborah Brodie
as well.
L. R. R.

Library of Congress Cataloging-in-Publication Data
Kanninen, Barbara J. (Barbara Joan)
A story with pictures / by Barbara Kanninen ;
illustrated by Lynn Rowe Reed. — 1st ed.
p. cm.
Summary: An author forgets to give her manuscript to
an illustrator who begins to paint whatever she herself
wants, making the author a character in the book, along
with a meddlesome duck and other creatures.
ISBN-13: 978-0-8234-2049-0 (hardcover)
[1. Illustration of books—Fiction.]
2. Authorship—Fiction.]
I. Reed, Lynn Rowe, ill. II. Title.
PZ7.K1278Sto 2007
[E]—dc22
2006019535

Designed by Yvette Lenhart

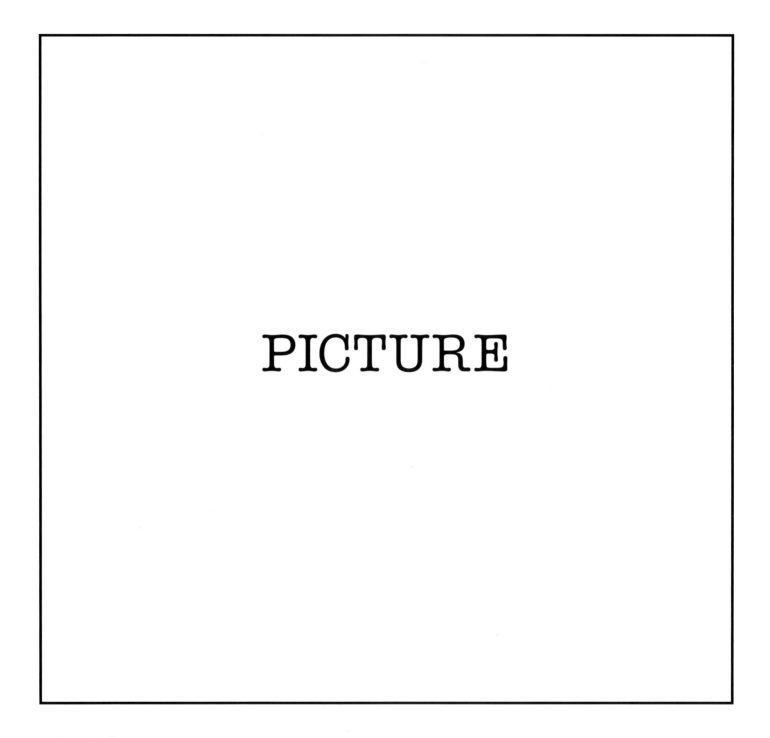

PICTURE

Ack! Where are the pictures?

This is supposed to be *A STORY WITH PICTURES*, not a story *WITHOUT* pictures. It says so right here in my manuscript.

My manuscript!

Oh no!

I forgot to give my manuscript to the illustrator. How will she know what to put in the pictures?

Oh dear. She obviously doesn't know. She painted a duck. There are no ducks in this story. I never write about ducks. Ducks are so . . .

OW!

Hey, I was going to say ducks are so cute.

But forget it.
You are not cute.

Your backpack is cute, though.
But why does it say,
What's supposed to be in this book?
I'm the only one who knows
that. I'm the author. You're a
duck; and may I remind you, I
never write about ducks . . .

MOO

or cows . . .
or trolls!

Run!

Oh no!
My manuscript!

HEE HEE

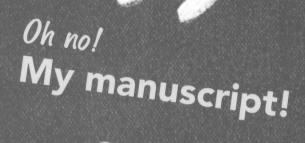

WHAT'S SUPPOSED TO BE IN THIS BOOK

What do I do now?
My manuscript flew
away and the illustrator
is painting all the
wrong pictures.

CHARACTER

Look at the slippers
she put on my feet.
I would NEVER wear
slippers like these
(though, hmm, they are
rather comfy).

Why are you pointing to your backpack again?
Okay, I'll look inside.

This note says *character*. Are you trying to tell me
the character that's *supposed to be in this book*?
Let me guess: a duck? a cow? a troll?

Ack! It's me.
But I'm not a character.
I'm the author. I would never
make myself a character.

Besides, characters are
supposed to have problems.
I don't have any problems.

Help!

I'm upside down!
These pictures are all wrong.

The illustrator has to stop now!

Wait! I didn't mean for her to stop halfway through the picture!

CHARACTER

Hey, Duck. Something
fell out of your backpack.
What does it say?

Excuse me? I know exactly what's supposed to happen in this book, and this is not supposed to happen!

That's it.
This is undignified.
I need to jump out
of this book and talk
to the illustrator
about these pictures. . . .

Ooops. I guess that wasn't an exit. Maybe over here . . .

BONK!

Hey, I can't get out. I'm stuck inside this book! The illustrator won't let me out of my own book.

Sigh. You again.
What do you want
to show me?

SETTING

Setting, huh?
Well, if I'm going to be
stuck inside this book,
I'd sure like the illustrator
to paint a nice setting.
Maybe a Parisian café . . .

or a tropical island . . .

She painted a
giant anthill?

Ahhhh!

Help, Duck!
Show me what setting is supposed to be in this book. Anything would be better than a giant anthill.

Huh? The setting is the inside of this book? But this is boring, and this is supposed to be the page that's most exciting: the point in the story where the character takes action.

You know, before I lost my manuscript, I was in charge of this book. If I wanted something exciting to happen, all I had to do was write about it.

That gives me an idea. Duck, do you have a pencil and paper?

There. Now, run this scene over to the illustrator. She'll know what to do.

**Wow! That was exciting.
How about this?**

I have another idea. Do you think the illustrator can paint moon shoes? I've always wanted to . . . try moon shoes.

Check out these moon shoes. I'm going to bounce all the way to the moon. BOING!

I can't believe it. I'm in space. I'm swashbuckling. I'm one cool character. Boy, oh boy, if I were the author of this book, I'd write about ME!

Where's the swashbuckling?
Where's the space travel?
Where's the . . . duck?
I can do better than this.
Where's your backpack?
Thank you, little guy.

Solution to problem:

Author returns to Earth (boing!), slips into her comfy slippers, and hammers away at a new story about an author who has no idea what's supposed to happen in her book.

She calls it A STORY WITH PICTURES...

and she puts a duck in it.